Toppling

Toppling

SALLY MURPHY

ILLUSTRATIONS BY
RHIAN NEST JAMES

CANDLEWICK PRESS

Text copyright © 2010 by Sally Murphy
Illustrations copyright © 2010 by Rhian Nest James

First U.S. edition 2012

Library of Congress Cataloging-in-Publication Data is available.

Library of Congress Catalog Card Number pending

ISBN 978-0-7636-5921-9

BVG 17 16 15 14 13 12
10 9 8 7 6 5 4 3 2 1

Printed in Berryville, VA, U.S.A.

This book was typeset in Garamond.
The illustrations were done in pen and watercolor.

Candlewick Press
99 Dover Street
Somerville, Massachusetts 02144

visit us at www.candlewick.com

For Helen and Sharon,
and all who live with cancer
S. M.

For Alexis and Lucien
R. N. J.

Chapter

Okay.
One last domino.
I inch my way back to the start—
carefully bend and
flick.
One after another,
tiles clack as they cascade
in a perfectly timed topple.
Clink
clink
clink clink clink.
In just seconds,
the last tile falls.

Yes!

I punch the air in satisfaction.
Not the biggest or cleverest
domino pattern I've laid out,
but it's always satisfying
when it works.

What are you doing, nerd boy?

My sister, Tess, is at my bedroom door.
*Mom'll kill you if she finds out
you're playing nerd games
instead of getting ready for school.*

Johnboy!
Mom yells from the kitchen, right on cue.
She always calls me Johnboy,
even though my name is just plain John.
Sometimes I like it,
but other times
(like when my friends are around)
I wish she wouldn't call me that.
It sounds babyish—
probably 'cause it's what she called me
when I *was* a baby.
Johnboy!
Are you ready to go?
Tess smirks,
but I don't care.

Almost! I call back,
throwing on my polo shirt.
Quickly I push the dominoes
into their crate,
hoping Mom won't hear the clink of tiles.

Some kids collect model cars
or airplanes
or stamps
or video games.
I collect dominoes.
I have thousands of them
in big crates under my bed:
little black tiles with white dots
and little white tiles with black dots—
made for an old game
that I've never really played.
Instead I like to watch them topple.
Tess says it's not normal
to spend so much time
arranging little tiles
just to make them fall over,
but I ignore her.
Maybe I'm not normal
but I'm happy.
If Tess is normal,
then that's something I don't want to be.

I'd like to play dominoes
all day, every day,
but Mom won't let me.
She seems to think other things
are important
like eating
and sleeping
and school.
Actually, I don't mind those things, really—
especially eating.
It's just that dominoes are better.
I tell her I could do without school.
Toppling dominoes teaches me
lots of skills
like math
and design
and patience.

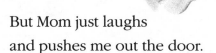

But Mom just laughs
and pushes me out the door.

School can be pretty lame,
but at least I get to see my friends—
especially Dominic.
Dominic Fraser likes rugby
and soccer
and cricket.
He likes reading funny books
and motorbike magazines.
He likes art,
but not math;
library,
but not science.
He has a dog named Butch
and five goldfish
and two parents,
but no brothers or sisters.
He has a computer of his own
and a Game Boy
and a remote-control helicopter.
He's fun
and funny
and honest
and pretty cool.

And he's my best friend.
And not just because
his name sounds like *domino*.
We first became friends
way back in kindergarten
when I wet my pants
and he didn't tell anyone.
Of course, we don't talk
about that now.
Five years later, I'm still embarrassed
about that day,
and since then
we've found lots of better things
to share,
like computer games
and jokes
and stuff.

Our other friends are
Joseph
and Christian
and Tran.

Joseph is super smart.
He knows everything
there is to know
about math
and science
and stuff like that.

Christian isn't so smart,
but he's funny.
He makes jokes
about anything
and everything
and keeps us
entertained
even at school—
which isn't easy.

Tran is pretty smart,
but he'd do better
in school if it was in Vietnamese
because that's the language
he speaks at home.
His English is pretty good,
but sometimes
if you mumble or talk too fast,
he looks at you strangely
and you know
he hasn't understood what
you've just said.

Me, I'm not smart
or funny
or from far away.
I'm just me.

Chapter

It's not great having to head back to school
after two weeks of vacation,
but it's cool being back with the gang.
Being in a group like ours
is great.
At recess
and lunch
and in class
you always have someone to sit with
or talk to
or just hang out with.
You always get chosen for a team
during PE,
and you have friends
who remind you about homework
and notes
and even practice after school.
Miss Timms calls us "the gigglers"
because on the first day
we couldn't stop laughing.
It's not a cool name
for a group of fifth-grade boys,
but it sounds okay
when Miss Timms says it.

Ky Johnson calls us "the dorks."
He's just jealous because
he's not in our group.
We don't want bullies.
Since he came halfway through last trimester,
he's mainly hung out by himself.
Lara Lewis calls us nothing.
She'd prefer we didn't exist—
she thinks all boys are pains
except for Brandon.
Brandon and his friends
play tennis and soccer and swim.
They have surfboards
and skateboards,
and when they're not at school,
they wear all the latest surf clothes.
Lara thinks Brandon is hot.
So does Brandon.

The only one in our class who *is* hot
is Lily.
She is pretty
and funny
and doesn't make girlie eyes at Brandon
like the other girls do.
But she sometimes smiles
at me and the guys
when we make jokes.

She's the next best thing
about school
after my buddies—
but I've never told anyone that.

Miss Timms likes projects.
First trimester she made us do a project
on ancient civilizations.
Last trimester it was about
the environment.
Dominic and I did a big diorama
about recycling.
This trimester, though,
Miss Timms has a surprise.
We can do our project on
(drum roll, please)
anything.
That's right:
anything we like.
Except
(there's always an *except*)
if it's X-rated or dangerous.

That's not fair, Ky mumbles.
I whisper to Dominic,
*Maybe Ky wants to blow up the school
in the buff.*
That's X-rated
and *dangerous,*
but I'm not sure he hears me.
I try not to think about Ky in the buff
and instead tune in to what
Miss Timms is saying.
We have to research
and report on our subject
in a three-minute speech
with props or posters.
Lara wants to do cats,
Lily wants to do Shakespeare,
Brandon wants tennis,
five people want horses,
and two the Grand Prix.
Other people are already
chewing their pencils
or their fingernails
as they worry about
choosing a good topic.

I already know what I want to do:
dominoes.
I wonder what Dom will do,
but then I realize
Dominic isn't really listening
to Miss Timms.

He's rubbing his face
with shaking hands.
I watch for a moment then nudge him.
Are you okay? I ask.
He doesn't answer
except to groan
and throw up technicolor puke
all over his desk.

Ewwww, says Lara Lewis.
That's gross!
Miss Timms looks green,
but she takes charge.
John, take Dom to the nurse
and ask if Mrs. Twiddle can come
with a bucket and sponge.
The rest of you, remain seated.
Dom walks slowly
and doesn't talk.
I keep pace
and watch beads of sweat
form on his forehead.
He looks like
a walking zombie.

At recess Ky is full of it.
Did you see dumb Dom?
That was so gross, he cries.

He runs around making throw-up noises
and grossing out the girls,
who cover their faces
and tell him to get lost.
No one is laughing,
but Ky doesn't care.
Tran and Christian and Joseph sit with me.
We try to ignore Ky,
but I see Christian's fists
bunch and unbunch
as his angry eyes
follow Ky around the playground.
We don't talk about Dom,
but I'm thinking of his pale face
and how embarrassed he must feel
about puking in front of everyone.
The classroom stinks
of vomit and disinfectant,
so after recess we're playing outdoor games
while the room airs out a bit.
At least there's something good
about Dom's chuck-fest.

When we line up to go back inside,
I see Dom and his mom
leaving school.
She's taking him home.
Dom's face is as white
as the dots on my black dominoes.
His mom frowns
as she carries his bag
and walks slowly beside him.

Something tells me
Dom won't be back at school
for a few days.
He looks like death warmed over.

Chapter

Dom might have been gone for two hours,
but we can still smell him in the classroom.
Miss Timms wrinkles her nose
as she comes in after lunch.
The windows have been open
since before recess
but the room still stinks.
I think we'll go and work in the library,
she says.
Bring your things.
In the library she gives us time
to start researching our projects.
Lara finds a book about cats.
Lily heads straight for the literature section.
Brandon finds a tennis book.
The horse people fight over
the three horse books.
There isn't a book about dominoes.
Am I the only person in the world
who likes toppling?

What are you doing, John?
asks Miss Timms.
Ky laughs.
He can't work
without his little friend, miss.
Miss Timms and I both ignore him.
I tell her there are no books on my topic.
You can try the Internet then.
Cool.
The second best thing I like to do
after domino toppling
is use the computer.
While the computer starts up,
I watch my friends working.
Christian wants to do something funny
and is searching for a book about comedy.
Tran wants to do shadow puppets.
He says his grandfather
always talks about them.
But Joseph doesn't know what to do.
He wanders the library aimlessly.
Joseph is the smart one,
but his grade won't be too good
if he doesn't have a topic.

Lucky he has all trimester.
Finally I am logged in.
I type *domino toppling*
into the search engine,
and soon I'm lost
in reading about my favorite hobby.
This free-choice project could be fun.

Here are some things
you may not know about dominoes.
Dominoes are little tiles
(also called bones)
that have dots on them.
Mostly they have between
one and six dots at each end,
but sometimes one or both ends
will be blank.
Dominoes are related to dice
and were invented by the Chinese.
Dominoes were made for a game
where you match ends
with the same number of dots,
but I think dominoes are
much more fun for toppling.

*   *   *

How was your first day back?
Mom asks at dinnertime.
She always likes to ask about our days
over dinner,
but then growls if we talk
with our mouths full.
Okay, I say.
Dom threw up all over his desk —
Tess groans.
Please! I'm eating.
Heh-heh.
I am glad I've put her off her dinner.
Maybe she'll leave more
French fries for me.

Is he okay? asks Mom.
I tell her that he went home
looking white
and how we couldn't use the classroom
because it was
all stinky
from the puke.
You should
have smelled it!

It's good to see Tess's face
when I say that,
but then I think of Dom
and how terrible he looked
and wonder if it's okay
to make fun of what happened.

Instead I change the subject
and tell them all about my project.
Sounds great, says Dad.
You could set up a topple
to show them how it works.
Good idea.
Pity it's not a group project this time.
It would be cool to do a topple with Dom.

Chapter

I don't expect to see Dom
at school for a day or so,
but when Monday comes
and he's still not there
I start to worry.
So do our friends.
I tried to call him, says Christian.
But no one answered the phone.
Tran went over to Dom's house,
but there was no car in the driveway
and no one came to the door.
We don't know what to do.
None of us has ever disappeared before.
Maybe we should ask Miss Timms, I say.
But we don't need to,
because when we go in to class
Miss Timms is wearing her serious face.

Usually she's all smiley and happy,
but when she needs to warn
or remind
or complain,
she wears her serious face.
She's wearing it now.
But it's different today.
Most times the serious face
doesn't go all the way to her eyes,
so we know that
she isn't really all that annoyed or upset.
This time, though, you can see
the seriousness in her eyes.
When she speaks,
I start to understand why.
Class, she says,
I have something to tell you.
Are we going on a field trip, miss?
Ky calls.
Shhh, says Lily.
She has seen Miss Timms's look, too.
Miss Timms ignores them both
and clears her throat.

Your friend Dom—
Ky guffaws.
Brandon pretends to cough.
I glare at them both
as I grip the front of my seat.
I can tell Miss Timms is going to say
something bad.
Your friend Dominic is not very well . . .
Is he still throwing up, miss?
Ky laughs.
Christian's chair is thrust back
and he's halfway out of it
when Miss Timms raises her voice.
That's enough, Ky!
Your thoughtless comments
are not appreciated.
I hear some gasps.
Did Miss Timms—
calm Miss Timms
nice Miss Timms
happy Miss Timms—
just yell at Ky?

Ky's mouth hangs open
like he's trying to catch a fly.
Brandon is snickering.
He doesn't like Ky either.
I don't think anyone does.
But Joseph and Christian and Tran and I
are waiting.
We want to know—
need to know—
what's wrong with Dom.

When everyone settles down,
Miss Timms tries again.
Unfortunately, Dominic is still not well.
Actually—
she pauses and glances at me
before looking away—
he's really very ill.
He's in the hospital.
We don't know when he'll be
back at school.
Ky is snickering again.
This time Christian makes it out of his chair,
but Miss Timms stops him.

Sit down, Christian.

Ky! I'll speak to you in the corridor.

Now.

Ky tries to keep a straight face
as he goes outside with Miss Timms.
Inside the room, people are buzzing,
wondering what's wrong with Dominic.
Their comments drift around me.

I went to the hospital once . . .

Maybe he's got . . .

Maybe he's . . .

Might be dying . . .

I don't know who said that,
but it's what I'm thinking, too.

I spent some time at the hospital last year.
My grandpa was really sick.
He had tubes
in his arms, his nose, his stomach,
and machines that beeped and pinged
and did everything for him.
Even breathe.
All we could do was sit and look
or whisper secrets that we didn't think
he'd hear.
I hated that hospital,
and I hated seeing Grandpa like that.
Is that how Dom looks now?
I watch Joseph and Tran
trying to calm Christian down.
I should go over there, too,
but I can't make my legs work.
What's wrong with my buddy?
My best friend?
I see Lily looking my way.
She gives me a sad kind of smile
as if she's trying to say she understands.
Finally, Miss Timms comes back in.
Alone.

Perhaps Ky has been sent
to the principal's office.
He spends lots of time there.
Now, where was I?
she says brightly
as if nothing is wrong.
But her voice is high,
her face is flushed,
and she still doesn't want to look at me.
Are there any questions?
Joseph's hand goes up.
What's wrong with Dom exactly? he asks.

Miss Timms frowns
and says she doesn't know,
but I think she's lying.
We just know
he needs an operation.
When we know more, we will tell you.
I stare at Miss Timms,
willing her to tell the truth.
It doesn't work.
Okay, fifth grade.
As Miss Timms writes on the board
and people open their books,
I am lost in thoughts of Dom.
What sort of operation cures throwing up?
Will it hurt?
Will he be okay?
When the recess bell rings,
I have no idea what it is we've been doing.
My mind is numb
and my legs, too.
I trudge outside to our usual spot.
The others are there waiting.
We don't say much.

Christian is still glaring at Ky,
who is sitting by himself.
The rest of the class is all off
kicking soccer balls
or giggling about boys
or raiding the library
or swapping granola bars.
We just sit, nibbling at our snacks
as if they're cardboard.
This is no good, says Tran.
*We need to know what is wrong
with Dominic.*

He's right,
but who'll tell us the truth?
Dom would, if he was here.
We tell each other everything.
Or maybe not *everything*—
I've never told the others
how I feel about Lily.
But mostly we're honest with one another.
I know that Joseph's scared of snakes
and that Tran hates violence.
I know that Christian's twin brother died
when they were born.
And I know that Dom—
well, I bet I know everything
about Dom.
Except what's wrong with him.
I'll get my mom to ask, I say.
She knows Dom's mom.
Having a plan helps a bit.
We're still quiet as we head back to class,
but at least we've got an idea
of how to find out.

Of all the domino patterns I do,
the spiral is the hardest.
You have to start in the middle,
then work outward,
with the domino line
circling like a snail.
It takes time and patience
to get it perfect.
Oh, and strong knees.
Mom says I'll end up with calluses
from all the time I spend kneeling and
crawling around
trying to get the setup just right.
This afternoon, though,
a spiral is helpful.
An hour spent painstakingly setting up
on the family-room floor
is an hour I don't need to be thinking
about Dom
and what might be wrong.

Finally I have it.
Three hundred tiles ready to go.
It's almost too good to mess up,
but I will.
I tip the first tile and
listen to the reassuring
clink clink clink
as the dominoes fall
in perfect timing
right to the last one.
Yes!

As always, I punch the air,
but it doesn't feel as great as usual.
I wish Dom could have seen the spiral.
Dom is not quite as crazy
about toppling as I am,
but he's happy to help
or to watch the dominoes fall.

I wonder when he'll get to watch again.
I kick at the fallen dominoes,
and they slide across the floor.
Maybe I should pack them up
before Mom gets home.

Too late.
I hear the front door open and close.
Hi, guys! I'm home.
Mom comes down the hallway and stops
when she sees my mess.
I see her struggling with whether
or not to growl.
She must decide "not."
Hi, Johnboy.
How was your day?
I swallow, suddenly unsure
how to ask her about Dom.

Maybe I don't really want to know.
But Mom is waiting,
so I decide to get it all out.
Crap, I say.
My day was crap.
Something is wrong with Dom.
Wrong? Mom stops still.
What do you mean?
I tell her about Dom still being
gone from school
and what Miss Timms said.
I don't tell her about the empty desk
or the empty spot in our group.
What's wrong with him, Mom?
Mom sighs.
Sounds bad, she says.
But maybe it's just his appendix
or something.
I'll see what I can find out.
Later — after dinner.
I brought home takeout!
Funny that I hadn't even smelled
the fried chicken until now.

When kids know stuff,
they usually blurt it out—
even bad stuff.
Did you see that guy on TV last night
who got blown up?
Mom and Dad had a big fight yesterday.
Tony loves Tracey.
Ky has a big wart on his butt.
(Actually I've never heard anyone say that
about Ky—
but I wish I had.
It'd be funny.)
But when adults know things,
you can see them worrying
about how to say it
and how much to tell you.
Just like Miss Timms today
and Mom now,
when she comes into my room
and sits at the end of my bed.
Dad has followed
and is standing in the doorway,
looking like he'd rather be watching TV.

Mom's eyes are red, and she has a tissue
clutched in her hand.
I can tell she's been crying,
and I know that
I'm not going to like
what she has to say.
I really look at Mom
to show her I'm ready to listen,
even if she's not ready to speak.
I wait.
Johnboy, she begins,
but her voice wobbles and she stops,
puts a hand on my shoulder, and sobs.
Tears trickle down her cheeks
and plop on her lap.
I want to hug her
to tell her it will be okay.
But I don't really think it will be.
Still, I have to know.
I put my hand on hers
and wait some more.
Dad comes closer and puts his hand
on her shoulder.

She gulps, sniffs, and tries again.
Dominic is in the hospital.
He is very sick.
Very sick indeed.
He has—
I watch Mom swallow,
afraid to meet my eyes—
He has a tumor.
She looks at me—
He has cancer.

My head whirls.
Cancer is bad.
Cancer is really bad.
People die from cancer.
Dom might die.
My best friend might die.
I want to ask a million questions,
but when I open my mouth,
nothing comes out.
Maybe this is what they mean in books
when they say someone is at a loss for words.
I've never been at a loss for words before.
But what can I say about my friend
who has cancer?

Dominic Fraser is eleven years old.
He's my friend.
He likes rugby
and soccer
and cricket.
He likes reading funny books
and motorbike magazines.
He likes art,
but not math;
library,
but not science.
He has a dog named Butch
and five goldfish
and two parents,
but no brothers or sisters.
He has a computer of his own
and a Game Boy
and a remote-control helicopter.
He is fun
and funny
and honest
and pretty cool.
And he has cancer.

Chapter

Sometimes when bad stuff happens,
you can't go to sleep,
and when you do, you toss and turn,
but things seem better in the morning.
Sometimes, but not this time.
This time I wake up
and right away
know that things are not better.
Not for me
and not for Dominic, either.
I imagine him in the hospital
waking up.
Is his mom with him?
His dad?
Is a nurse there, taking his temperature?
Or is he all alone in his hospital room,
which is nothing like his room at home?
Mom is calling me to get ready for school,
but I don't want to go.
What's the point?
Maybe I can pretend to be sick.
When I think of Dom, my stomach churns.
Maybe I really am sick.
But Dad is there in my doorway.

I know how you feel, Johnboy.
No, he doesn't.
But staying home won't help things.
You need to carry on as usual
for your sake and for Dom's.
How will my going to school help Dom?
Can I learn stuff for him?
Do his project for him?
Goof around on the playground for him?
I don't think so.
Sometimes parents just don't get it.

I shuffle across the playground.
I kick a rock and hear it crash into a trash can.
In the corridor outside our classroom
my friends are waiting—
Tran and Christian and Joseph,
but not Dom.
I can see from the looks they give me
that they already know,
but I have to ask anyway.
Did you hear about Dom?
They nod.
It sucks, says Tran.

Tran never talks like that.
Cancer is very bad.
And my mother said he's having
an operation
to remove his kidney.
I nod.
Can you live without a kidney?
asks Christian.
I wondered that, too
when Mom told me last night,
but now I know that you have two kidneys—
unless one is full of cancer
and has to be removed.
Why didn't Miss Timms tell us the truth?
asks Joseph.
As if she knows we are talking about her,
Miss Timms appears at the classroom door.
I glare at her—
angry she didn't tell us yesterday.
She sees my glare,
but instead of being upset, she looks sad
as she walks over.

Hello, boys, she says.
*I guess your parents
have told you about Dom.
There is nothing I can say
that will make you feel better,
but just know
that when you want to talk,
I am here
and so is Trish.*

Trish? The school counselor?
She talks to naughty kids
and upset kids.
Why would she talk to us?
But when I look at my friends' faces,
I realize that right now
we *are* the upset kids.
What are we going to do?

In class we make get-well cards for Dom,
even though we don't know
if he will get well.
Some kids make a lot of effort
with glitter and glue and markers.
Other kids rush and scribble
just to get it done.

Do they know
that Dom might die?
Miss Timms has still not told them
the truth.
My card is perfect.
I use black paper
and mark Dom's name on the front
in white dots
so it looks like his name's on a domino.
But when I open it up, I don't know what
to write inside.
Get well?

A command to do something
he already wants to do?
Wish you were here?
That's lame.
In the end I just write, **Miss you**,
and hope he'll know it's true.

The cards are collected,
but when Miss Timms gets to Ky's desk,
he is empty-handed.
I don't wanna send a card, he tells her.
He's not even my friend.
Miss Timms tells Ky to stay in at recess,
but there's no point.
He'll always be nasty,
and he'll never understand.
How would he know
what it's like to miss somebody?
He has no friends to miss.

Out on the playground,
Christian mutters about Ky
and what he'd like to do to him.
Joseph tells him to calm down,
but I can tell he's mad, too.
Then after recess, I see something
that makes me think.
A new card on the pile
on Miss Timms's desk.

As I walk past,
I pick it up for a peek.
A card from Ky.
Inside he has written:
I hop you get betta.
He is a terrible speller,
but he's written something nice.
I wonder if Miss Timms made him do it.
I put the card back on the pile
just as Miss Timms turns around
from the whiteboard.
Her lips twitch, but she says nothing.

Chapter

Sometimes having a hobby
can help take your mind off things.
Every day after school,
I hurry home
and build new domino patterns:
spirals
bridges
squares
stairs.
Up and down the hallway,
all around the family room,
even one that starts in my room
up on my desk.
Hours and hours of crawling and setting
and grumbling when it goes wrong
and cheering when it goes right
and annoying my sister
when the dominoes are in her way.
Being busy helps a little bit,
but every night
I still ask Mom for news of Dom.

Phone calls are for Mom
or Dad
or Tess
or people we've never heard of,
but when the phone rings,
it's never someone asking for me.
Still, when it rings and no one else
is in the room,
I have to answer it
or Mom gets cross.
So when it rings on Friday night,
I pick it up.
Walmsley residence, John speaking, I say.
I know it sounds dumb,
but that's how Mom says I should
answer the phone.

John? It's me.
I don't have to ask who "me" is.
I'd know that voice anywhere,
even if it sounds more tired
and wobblier than I remember.
Dom! I shout. *How are you?*
then cringe
as I remember how dumb that must sound
to my friend with cancer.
But Dom pretends it's a normal thing
to ask.
Okay, he says. *I'm okay.*
But I'm stuck in the hospital and it's boring.
Can you come and visit?
Of course I can.
I've wanted to go all week,
but Mom said I had to wait.
Now Dom is asking, and I know
Mom will have to say yes.
We talk a little more without saying much,
then he puts his mom on to talk to mine.
Adult talk.
I don't care because tomorrow
I can go and see Dom.

Hospitals smell
like sickness
and flowers
and roast dinners
and medicine
and the stuff you use to scrub toilets.
Mostly they are quiet
except for the beeps of machines
and the shuffle of feet on the corridor floor
and the murmur of nurses at the front desk.
That's how I remember the hospital where
Grandpa was, anyway.
But Dom's hospital is not like that at all.
Except for the smells—
they're the same.
But this hospital is bright and colorful
with cutesy murals for the little kids
of clowns and butterflies and fish.
There is music playing.
Loudly.
While a boy with no hair beat-boxes.
His audience is a girl in a wheelchair
and a nurse in a blue dress
and a boy with sad eyes

in the opposite bed . . .
a boy who turns his eyes to me
and says my name as I come in.
I can't believe that it is Dom.

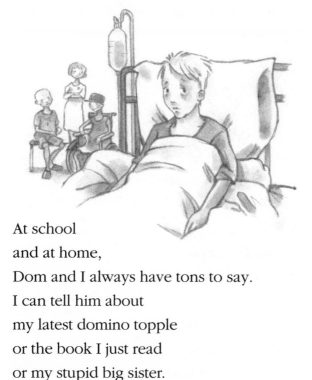

At school
and at home,
Dom and I always have tons to say.
I can tell him about
my latest domino topple
or the book I just read
or my stupid big sister.
He tells me
about his rugby practice
or the TV show he watched last night
or the new trick he's taught Butch,

and sometimes we don't need to talk.
We just hang out.
But here in the hospital,
the words are hard.
They're stuck behind the big lump
in my throat,
not wanting to come out.
The silence hangs between us
like a screen.
I can no longer hear the beat-box boy
or the nurses outside.
Just the terrible silence
of our search for words.
Finally Dom speaks.
It's good you came.
This place is full of sick people.
I laugh
and in a flash the silence is gone
and we can talk.
Are you okay? I ask.
I will be, he says.
But I don't know when.
He tells me about his cancer
and the operation to remove the tumor,

which was on his kidney.
So I just have one kidney, he says.
But that's better than having a tumor
growing inside me.
Now the tumor's gone,
and I have a big hole in my side
with staples to hold it closed,
and soon I will have no hair.

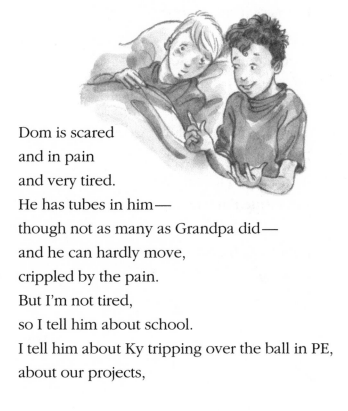

Dom is scared
and in pain
and very tired.
He has tubes in him—
though not as many as Grandpa did—
and he can hardly move,
crippled by the pain.
But I'm not tired,
so I tell him about school.
I tell him about Ky tripping over the ball in PE,
about our projects,

about my dominoes.
I even tell him that I think Lily is pretty,
but he tells me he already knew that.
Then Mom comes to find me.
I don't want to go
and Dom looks like he wants me to stay,
but he has to rest
and Mom promises him that
I can come again soon.
I turn to leave,
pretending I don't see
the tears in Dom's eyes.
But I do
and I see them in Mom's eyes, too.
I have no tears—
not on the outside.
But inside I'm bawling.

I think my friend
is dying.

Chapter

Back at school, Miss Timms
works us hard.
Fifth grade is an important year.
You must get ready for middle school.
She says more
about grades
and homework
and study skills,
but she could
be saying,
blah
blah
blah,
for all I care.
I want to ask
if staying alive
is part of the curriculum
and if Dom will be allowed
to come to middle school
after missing so much of fifth grade.
But I don't ask—
too scared of what the answers might be.

At first

our group seemed empty without Dom,

but now it seems almost normal.

Apart from that first day

when he puked,

Dom hasn't been here all trimester.

One recess Christian makes a joke

and we all laugh,

and I forget for a moment

that Dom's supposed to be here

laughing with us.

Until Tran says,

Dom would like that joke,

and we stop laughing.

But I remember Dom laughing

and telling jokes of his own,

and suddenly I know that he needs jokes.

Maybe we could help Dom to laugh, too.

Let's go and see him together

and tell him our jokes.

Soon we are laughing again

as we practice the jokes we'll tell Dom.

Dom is not in his bed in the hospital.
Instead a stranger's there.
A stranger with no hair
and sunken eyes.
Hi, guys, the stranger says,
and I remember
how I didn't recognize Dom
the first time I visited.
Hi, Dom! I say,
hoping I sound enthusiastic.
Joseph bounds over to the bed,
but Christian shuffles.
He's lost his voice, just like I once did.
Tran holds out the fruit
his mother made him bring.
I thought chocolate would be better
but Mom thinks apples are best
for the hospital.
Dom smiles weakly and puts the apple
on his bedside table.

You guys look terrible, he says.
He knows how to break the ice,
and soon we're laughing
and telling our jokes,
and a nurse has to ask us to quiet down
because the beat-box boy is sleeping.
But I don't think any of us
are laughing inside.

The day of our speeches is getting nearer.
I'm making index cards
shaped like dominoes,
and my list of domino facts
is getting longer.
Now I have to come up with
a good opening
and a great conclusion.
Miss Timms says we must
start and end with a bang
if we want people to remember
our speeches.

Tran is busy making
a shadow puppet.

Christian is practicing his jokes.
We've heard them a thousand times,
but we'll still laugh
at the right times
so that the class will laugh, too.

Joseph won't tell us
what his speech is about,
but I know he is
working very hard
to get it right.
It must be about
something special.

I've seen Ky working hard on his project
whenever Miss Timms gives us time.
It's the only time
he seems to do any work.
During math and spelling
he goofs off,
calling out dumb things
and annoying Miss Timms—
and the rest of us.
But when we work on our projects,
he is quiet.

Chapter

Dom is allowed home
in between chemo sessions.
When he says "allowed,"
it sounds like the doctors
are doing him a favor,
like releasing him from prison
or letting him go on a school field trip
instead of him going back
to the place he lives.
Home.
The hospital ward might have
bright colors
and loud music
and even laughter (sometimes),
but it is still a hospital ward.

So, he's at home,
and I go to see him after school.
He asks me about Joseph and Christian
and Tran.
He asks about Miss Timms
and our projects.
He even asks about Ky and Brandon.
He must be really bored.
He wants to come back,
but his mom is worried
that it will make him worse.
I look at his skinny arms,
his bald head,
and his face drained of color,
and wonder if it is possible
for him to be worse.
I wish he could come back
for a visit,
but I really wish
he could come back for good.

Before I leave, Dom motions for me
to come closer.
I sit on the edge of his bed
and know he is going to say
something important.
I'm glad you came, John, he says.
And I'm glad we can still goof around.
I'm so sick of people treating me
like a baby
or, worse, as if they think I am going to die.
My stomach plunges.
That word makes me shudder,
and before I know it
I ask him,
Are you going to die, Dom?
As soon as I've said it,
I wish I could take it back.
But Dom doesn't flinch.
He looks me straight in the eye
and answers.
I don't know, he says.
But sometimes, when they give me chemo,
I shiver

and puke
and can't even stand.
When that happens,
I wish I was dead.
But then, when all that is over
and I can come home
and be with Mom and Dad
or read a good book
or talk with you and the guys,
I remember that I want to live
for a long, long time.
I do not answer Dom
for a while.
I am stunned
that my friend sometimes wishes
he was dead
and glad that he doesn't feel that way
all the time.
But mostly I wonder
if the choice is even his.
So I tell him the only thing I can.
Well, I'm glad you're alive,
and I can't wait for you to get better.

When I get home,
I decide to set up a topple.
It'll take my mind off my talk with Dom.
But I'm halfway through setting it up
when Tess stomps through the house
and slams a door
and all my tiles fall over.

You idiot! I yell,
and kick the dominoes across the room.
You always ruin everything!
Tess opens the door
and pokes her head through.
Sooo-reeee, she singsongs.
It was an accident.
Chill, little bro.
But I don't want to chill.
My topple is ruined
because of my stupid sister.

I start to collect my scattered tiles,
flinging them at the crate.
What's up, Johnboy?
Mom comes to see what the fuss is about.
She sits and watches me packing up.
Things are hard for you, John,
but yelling at your sister
won't help.
I sigh.
Maybe Mom is right,
but there is no one else to yell at.

Later, something strange happens.
Tess comes into my room
and flops herself on my bed.
I'm sorry about before, she says.
It really was an accident.
And I'm sorry about Dom, too.
She is blinking a lot.
It must be hard not knowing
if he'll be okay.

Then she gets up and leaves.
She doesn't wait for me to reply,
and I'm not sure I could.
Maybe Mom and Dad
made her apologize,
but I don't think so.
I think maybe even *Tess*
is worried about Dom.

Chapter

The trimester has flown by,
and now it is speech day—
the second-to-last day before the break.
The morning is filled
with talks about horses
and tennis.
Everyone laughs at Christian's jokes
and *oob*s at Tran's puppet,
but soon it will be my turn, and
my palms are sweaty.
I give up my lunchtime
to set up my topple on Miss Timms's desk.
It is not the biggest topple I've ever done,
but it has a ramp and a drop
and will finish my speech nicely.
Miss Timms makes everyone
come in calmly
so the dominoes won't fall.
Slow down, Ky, she orders.

When everyone is seated, I begin.
My sister thinks I'm a dork,
but I don't care
because one day I am going to
make a world record, I say.
I'm not sure if I have begun with a bang.

Brandon is smirking.
Ky is looking at his note cards.
But Joseph and Christian and Tran
are listening
and Lily is, too.
I explain all about the world record
and how it takes millions of dominoes
and lots of people to set up
a topple like that.
Then I talk about how much fun
toppling is
and about the different patterns
you can make
and the accessories you can use.
And all the time I am looking to see
people's reactions.
I have said enough.
I ask everyone to sit
where they can see.
Tiles topple up a ramp,
clink clink clink
to a marble waiting at the
top of the towers.

Plop!
It drops
right where it should,
and the dominoes continue to topple
just as I hoped
around the desk,
up and down the ramp.
It takes only seconds,
but it feels longer,
and I have time to see that
everyone is watching closely.
Finally, the last line of dominoes falls.
The last topple activates the toy cannon,

and out pops a little white flag
inscribed with a word:
Bang!
Everyone laughs and claps,
and I smile,
and Joseph
and Tran
and Christian
all high-five me.
They help me pack up,
and I go back to my desk,
feeling glad
my talk is over.

There are just two more talks to go—
Joseph's and Ky's.
I have kept these two till last,
says Miss Timms,
because they are very serious.
Please listen politely,
even if there are no dominoes
or horses
or tennis rackets.
I want to listen.
I am intrigued.
Joseph makes his way to the front.
He has not given us one clue
what his speech is about.
Joseph unrolls his poster
and *ahems* nervously.
My talk, he says
as he straightens the poster,
is about cancer.

The poster has no special fonts
or sparkles.
It doesn't even have any words.
All it has is a big photo
of our friend Dom.
Everyone is listening.
Joseph tells us
all he can about cancer
and tumors
and chemotherapy.

I can't help thinking
that a few months ago
this speech would have been boring,
but now it's interesting
because it's stuff we want to know.
Joseph finishes his speech
with his own bang.
People die from cancer, he says.
But not always.
It is up to us to help them live,
any way we can.
Everyone else claps,
but I stand up,
and it is my turn to high-five Joseph
as he walks back to his desk.

Miss Timms crumples a tissue
as she stands up.
Thank you, Joseph, she says.
That was very informative.
Now it is your turn, Ky.

I don't want to hear Ky's talk.
It'll be about something dumb like cars
or wrestling.
But Miss Timms is watching us all,
so I pretend to be interested.
Ky has his own poster
and, like Joseph, he also has a photo.
But I don't recognize this man.
He has brown hair
and laughing eyes
and a tattoo on his shoulder.
He might be someone famous,
but I don't know who.
Ky is just standing there
holding the poster.
Go on, Ky, says Miss Timms.
We're ready.

*   *   *

This is my dad, says Ky.
Now I am listening.
I have never seen Ky's dad before.
Ky lives with his mom and
his two little sisters.
I see them sometimes waiting for him
at the school gate.
But as I listen to Ky's speech,
I find out why
I've never seen his dad.
Ky's speech is about cancer, too.
About how his dad had leukemia
and got very sick.
Ky tells us
about the months his dad spent in bed
and in and out of the hospital.

He tells us how his dad died
while Ky and his family
sat at his bedside
and about how they had to
sell their house and move.
I have never heard Ky say so much.
Miss Timms has tears on her cheeks
and so does Ky,
but no one laughs or points.
Ky finishes his speech with a bang, too.
Now Dominic has cancer, he says.
Dominic isn't my friend,
but he is a real person
and he is very sick.
We should all hope
that he gets better.
I do.

I have never high-fived a bully before,
and if you had told me yesterday
that I would do it today,
I would have laughed.
Loudly.

But when Ky walks past me,
I stand up and do just that
and he smiles.
Then Joseph and Tran and Christian
high-five him, too.
Some other kids copy us.
It was a sad speech,
but it seems right to be happy
that Ky shared his story now,
when we need to hear it.

Miss Timms has one more bang
to finish with.
Thank you all for your speeches, she says.
It is hard to get up and talk
in front of everyone
and I thank you all for working so hard.
As if we had any say in it.
But she is right—
it has been an interesting day.
Now I have some news for you.
Something exciting.
A field trip, miss? asks Ky.
Sometimes I think he has
field trips on the brain.
No, Ky, not today.
But maybe one day.
She smiles.
No, what I want to say
is that tomorrow
we are having a visitor.
Dominic is coming
to see us.

I feel ticked off.
Miss Timms has said Dom is a visitor
as if he doesn't belong here.
But then I realize what she has said.
Dom is coming to school.
That's cool!
Miss Timms warns us that
Dom is very weak
and looks different.
I know all this and I don't care.
Dom is coming to school.
Tomorrow.
But then I wonder if *he* will care
that he looks different.
Will it be hard for him to show everyone
that he is bald?
Maybe there's something
we can do to help.
As the bell rings,
I call Christian and Joseph and Tran over.
Ky comes, too, and I let him listen.
Why not?

At home I don't set up a topple.
Instead I head to Tess's room.
I need your help, I say.
She frowns,
but when I tell her my plan,
she says she will help.
When Mom and Dad get home,
they are surprised to find us
laughing together
and even more surprised
to see what we have done.
When they laugh, too,
I know my plan is a good one.

I don't like school,
but today I can't wait to get there—
and not just because
it's the last day of the trimester.
Christian is waiting at the school gate,
and we laugh out loud
when we see each other,
then smile at Joseph
and Tran when they arrive.
Miss Timms smiles, too
when she sees us walk in.
And Lily gives me a huge grin.

Ky is late to school
and looks scared when
he comes into the room,
but everyone claps
and Miss Timms lets him move
to sit near us.
Soon we hear voices in the corridor,
and Dom's mom appears in the doorway.
She's brought Dom to school
but wouldn't let him come in alone.
At last Dom enters, walking slowly.
He looks around the room
until he sees me
and our friends
and Ky,
and then his mouth falls open.
His bald head is covered by a beanie.
But Joseph and Tran and Christian and Ky
and I
all have shiny bald heads, too
and as we lean forward,
he can read the message
we have written on our scalps.

I don't know if Dom will get well,
but I do know
that seeing his smile
in our classroom
has given me hope
and that seeing our bald heads
has done the same for him.
I am gentle as I rush to
give him a high five.

I do not want to see Dom topple.